IMAGOES

AN IMAGO SERIES SHORT STORY

N.R. WALKER

COPYRIGHT

BLURB

AN IMAGO SERIES SHORT STORY

When Jack receives a phone call from a colleague in the southeast of Tasmania with news of a newfound butterfly habitat, he and Lawson head off on another adventure.

It's not an easy trek to the location. The Franklin-Gordon National Park is famous for wild rivers, rainforests, and rocky cliff faces, and they'll need to hike and abseil—in the dead of winter—to get to the site.

It's no ordinary expedition because this is no ordinary butterfly, and Jack and Lawson aren't an ordinary couple.

Join Jack and Lawson on another quest in this short story of extraordinary butterflies and extraordinary love.

IMAGOES

N.R. WALKER

CHAPTER ONE

JACK

THE WIND WAS HOWLING OUTSIDE, sleet was coming down in a flurry of different angles, and I was grateful to be inside with a warm fire. Rosemary was asleep by the hearth and Brennan was on the couch, perched up with his lap table and a colouring book, his pencils in a perfectly organised row.

He was all of four years old now, with a better vocab than most adults. He wore little sweaters all the time and tidy pants, his hair combed to perfection, his manners as sweet as he was.

God, he was so much like his daddy.

Then, right on cue, Daddy came in through the back door, a burst of cold wind behind him. Closing the door, he let out a breath, unwound his scarf, and pulled off his beanie. He'd been mostly data collating in his butterfly house office. Given most butterflies were dormant in the winter, there wasn't much happening. But his work never stopped. "My word, it's abysmal out there," he mumbled, straightening his hair. He gave me a kiss on the cheek. "Dinner smells amazing."

"Beef stew with dumplings," I said, pulling the oven door down.

Lawson inhaled, his hand at my back. "I would marry you again if I could."

I chuckled and he went over to Brennan, sitting down beside him, put his arm around him and kissed the top of his head. "You finished work, Daddy?"

"I did. What are you working on there?"

"Colouring the sea turtle," Brennan replied. He took his work very seriously. "Did you save the butterflies today?"

Lawson smiled. "I sure did." Then he proceeded to point and explain the parts of the turtle's anatomy, and Brennan nodded, wide-eyed, soaking up every drop of information he could.

He was *so* much like his daddy.

They were just so cute, I could barely stand it. My heart was full, like it had been since the day I met Lawson, and then doubly so from the day we met Brennan. Our lives changed forever the day we officially became parents. We'd never been busier, more exhausted, sleep-deprived, and stretched thin between work and home. But we'd never been happier.

Lawson's butterfly research had been elevated to a whole other level, and while he was internationally acclaimed and famous within the lepidoptery world, he never let it go to his head. He never once made his work more important than mine or more important than our family. It wasn't even that he was humble about it. He just had no idea of his own brilliance. Don't get me wrong, he knew he was intelligent and good at what he did, but he never could see what all the fuss was about.

It was something I loved about him.

"Are we ready for dinner?" I asked.

Lawson smiled at me. "Absolutely. Brennan and I shall set the table."

Brennan neatly put his pencil in its place, closed the colouring book, then put his table tray squarely on the coffee table before he helped with the placemats and cutlery. It was like watching two Lawsons: one big, one small.

I put the casserole dish on the stovetop and walked over to them, taking Lawson's face in my hands and kissing him soundly on the lips, then placed a gentle kiss on the top of Brennan's head.

"What was that for?" Lawson asked, smiling but perplexed.

"You're both so cute, I couldn't help it."

Brennan giggled as he took his seat. "Dadda, you're silly."

So I tickle-kissed him again while he laughed and squirmed. Lawson plated up dinner and I poured everyone a glass of water, and like we did every night, we sat down for dinner. Lawson asked me about my day and we talked about the hazard-reduction plans I was implementing, given it was winter. Brennan had been at pre-school, so he had much to tell us about his day—and how, with a slightly sardonic rise of his cute little eyebrows, he was now allowed to use *safety* scissors—and Lawson told us of the data collation he'd been working on for the Australian Lepidopterist Society on the conservation of the purple copper butterfly: a rare butterfly in New South Wales that he'd been assisting on.

Talking about our day was our nightly ritual and one of my most favourite things in the world.

When we were packing up after dinner, my phone rang.

"Jack Brighton-Gale speaking."

"Hello Jack, this is Connor Tallis from Franklin-Gordon National Park. We've met a few times at State Park seminars."

I racked my brain . . . Connor, tall blond guy from the southwestern part of Tasmania. My national park was northeast, almost opposite corners of the state. But I remembered him. "Yes, mate. How's winter down your way?"

"Biting."

I chuckled. "I bet it is. What can I do for you?"

"Well, this is going to sound a bit odd. But I was hoping I could have a word with your husband, Lawson Brighton-Gale."

"Doctor Lawson Brighton-Gale," I corrected automatically.

Lawson smirked at that, but I had his attention.

"May I ask what this is in relation to?"

"Yeah sure," he replied. "We had some campers through last week and they'd done some abseiling and found their way into a cave formation in the cliffs there. I was talking to them when they got back, and one of them happened to mention something they found fascinating. There were butterflies and cocoon casings stuck to the roof of the cave."

I shot Lawson a look and he left the sink and walked over to me.

"Anyway," Connor went on. "Me and one of my guys went up and had a look. It's not an easy climb and it involves abseiling . . . but I found what they were talking about. I took photos and some of the old casings from the cave floor, and I found one dead butterfly. I brought it all back to document, you know, as we do." I nodded, though he couldn't see. It was procedure to document all fauna findings. "But I looked online and couldn't find anything even close. I was hoping your butterfly guy might be able to help."

I got that excited feeling in my belly. "I'll just put him on."

I handed my phone to Lawson. "Connor Tallis from Franklin-Gordon National Park. Found a butterfly."

Lawson made a face but took the phone. "Doctor Lawson Brighton-Gale speaking."

I left him to it and put Brennan in the bath and got him ready for bed. Lawson was still speaking to Connor and there was talk of photographs, and I could tell from the length of the conversation that Lawson was intrigued.

When I brought Rosemary in from her bedtime bathroom break, Lawson was off the phone but now staring intently at his laptop screen.

"What was it?" I asked. "Some never-seen-before discovery?" Which I said as a joke . . .

He looked up at me with wide-eyed excitement and that smile he reserved just for me and butterflies. And then he nodded. "Yes, Jack. I think it is."

He turned the laptop around so I could see, and there was a photograph of a small butterfly. The image wasn't great, but I could see it was pink with a band of black along the outer hindwings. "It's pink," I said. "I don't think I've ever heard you talk of a pink butterfly."

Lawson's excitement was contagious. "Because, technically, there is no such thing."

"Really?"

He shook his head. "Slight variations of purple and light refractions give the appearance of pink, but no."

I nodded toward the screen. "Could this be light refractions?"

"Possibly. The photo isn't great. But where they found the specimen is most interesting."

"How so?"

"In the end of a cave with no light. And these specimens are in the imago stage. In winter. Connor swore he saw them just two days ago." Lawson shook his head in wonder. "Jack, that's not right."

I grinned at him. A new butterfly. Well, another new butterfly. This was what dreams were made of. "Well, doctor, I do believe we just might need to go check it out."

***

"ARE you sure your sister and mum don't mind?" Lawson asked me for the tenth time. We were loading gear into the back of the four-wheel drive while my sister Poppy and my mother stood on the porch with Brennan.

"Lawson, my love," I said, trying to be patient. "I hadn't even finished asking if they could please come and look after him and they were already in the car on their way here. Mum left so fast she had to call my dad and tell him he was on his own for four days. That's how excited she was."

Lawson almost smiled, but it ended with a sigh. "I just don't like leaving him."

"I know. I don't either. But it's just four days. He has pre-school for two of those and Poppy has plans for one art-and-craft day and one biscuit-baking day. They will be more than fine. Plus, Rosemary's here. She'll watch over him."

He finally managed a smile at that. "Okay."

With a final round of hugs and goodbyes, we gave them a wave and made our way down the drive. It'd be a decent four-hour drive, given the drizzly weather. Lawson hadn't been too keen to go, but given he was more than certain this was a new species of butterfly, his love for the species won out over his dread of hiking and, God-forbid, abseiling.

But me? I couldn't wait.

Not just the hike and abseiling and seeing the Franklin-Gordon National Park again, but also for four days with Lawson.

Sure, we'd have Connor and two of his team with us. But this was the first time Lawson and I had been away together without Brennan in four years.

And yes, while I would miss our son terribly, he was in very capable hands and I was absolutely down for some one-on-one daddy time. Plus, hiking and butterflies are what we do.

Lawson was quiet for a while, his hands in his lap, and he did that fingertip-squeezing thing he tended to do when he was nervous. When he began to pat down his hair, I knew he was starting to freak out.

I reached over and took his hand, keeping it on his thigh. "Lawson, baby, what's wrong?"

He blinked and his face twitched a little and he huffed out a few breaths while he was trying to get his thoughts in order. "I hate that you know me so well."

I snorted. "No you don't."

He scowled and rolled his eyes. "This expedition, while very exciting, also involves a considerable hike through diffi-cult terrain and abseiling down a sheer rock cliff face. Not to mention the river systems. They call them the Wild Rivers for a reason." He swallowed hard. "I don't need to remind you of the incidents thus far in our expedition career, do I? The bushfire where we both almost got incin-erated, the cane-toad-toxicity incident where I almost died, the inland-taipan incident where you almost died, and the ankle incident in the Snowy Mountains." He shook his head. "I would offer to stay at base camp and allow you to go on my behalf, because I trust you to follow proper collation procedure, but the idea of you going by yourself makes me feel ill. Then if we both go, I fear if something should happen to both of us, leaving Brennan without either of his fathers, I just can't—"

"Whoa, okay," I said, squeezing his hand. His anxiety was much higher than I'd first realised. "Lawson, my love. Nothing bad is going to happen. I promise."

"Please do not promise the outcome of things for which you have no control."

Well, that was fair enough. You'd think I'd be used to how literal his brain was. "Okay. Your fears are understandable and justified. Sorry I tried to downplay them. The Franklin-Gordon National Park is as wild as it gets. But Lawson, this could very well be the find of your career."

"The Tillman Copper is the find of my career."

"*Another* find of your career," I amended. "Along with the African White-barred Emperor found in the Northern Territory *and* the conservation work you've done for the Ulysses in Queensland *and* the Purple Copper in New South Wales."

He huffed but said nothing.

"From the photographs and details Connor sent you, you're certain this could be a new species," I continued. "That's really big, Lawson. It's important you do this. What I can promise you is that we'll be prepared, we'll be safe, and this will be an incredible experience."

He sighed and conceded with a nod, though he relaxed a bit if the release of pressure on my hand was anything to go by.

"I just worry, that's all."

"I know you do. It's what makes you a wonderful dad."

His eyes met mine and his face softened. "You're a wonderful dad too."

I lifted his hand to my lips and kissed his knuckles. "Now why don't you go over the details and tell me everything you're thinking about this butterfly."

If there was one thing that could take his mind off any potential dangers or worries, it was the finer details of his work. And truthfully, I could listen to him talk about barometric pressure, the biotic factors, and the non-floral factors and how the fact they were located in a cave made this quite remarkable, but it raised a slew of negative-variable questions, which Lawson spoke about—at length—for the better part of an hour.

"To surmise, it's all ecological theories until I can see it and study it for myself . . ." He trailed away with a smile. "You know, the way you can manipulate me is as embarrassing as it is endearing."

I barked out a laugh. "I don't manipulate anything. I simply know how your very brilliant mind works. And sometimes that means to de-escalate a meltdown, you simply need to follow protocol. Once you see something as just procedural steps and routine, you're fine."

He stared at me for a long moment, then blinked. "De-escalate a meltdown?"

Oh, shit.

"Not a *melt*down, as such. More of a stress-fest, or if you need a few moments to collect your thoughts and take a breath, that's all." I cleared my throat. "Remember when I was endearing just a few seconds ago? That was nice."

He tried to glare at me but a smile won out. "You're still endearing. Though meltdown and stress-fest are two words I'd prefer not to hear again, thank you all the same."

I laughed and kissed his hand again. "And you've

abseiled before. It's not like we have to do white-water rafting to get there."

Lawson pursed his lips and glared out the windscreen. "If anyone mentions white-water rafting, even in jest, you will see a meltdown. And it will measure on the Richter scale. Just so you know."

I stifled another laugh. "Duly noted, thank you, doctor."

CHAPTER TWO

LAWSON

I DIDN'T KNOW what to expect when we met Connor. Jack had said he was a tall man, thirty-one-or-two years old, pleasant enough the few times he'd met him. They had spoken a handful of times over the years at their national park meeting and seminars, though Jack admitted to not knowing him well.

And Jack was right.

He was tall and pleasant . . . enough. He also had sandy coloured hair, a roguish smile, and a striking face. I'd have placed him on a beach with a surfboard before I likened him to inland rainforests and wild river systems kind of guy.

We met them in a car park at one of the many national park's hiking trails off the Lyell Highway. Connor was out of his vehicle as soon as we pulled up, huge smiles and strong handshakes, and my immediate reaction was to take a step back. He gave off loud cowboy extrovert vibes that were enough to make any introvert want to run and hide.

"G'day, Jack," he said brightly, shaking his hand. "And you must be Doctor Brighton-Gale."

Well, he'd learned that quickly after Jack had corrected

him on the phone, and now I had to correct him again, which was incredibly awkward. "Lawson's fine. Nice to meet you."

Two young off-siders had stepped out of the car, waiting to be introduced. They were mid-twenties, maybe. "This is Vince and Amy," Connor said. "They'll be coming along on the trip. Apart from being really good rangers, they can help us carry stuff."

Nice. Nothing like being called a pack mule in front of your peers.

I made a mental note to ask Jack what his parameters were when saying someone is "nice enough" and exactly what was the *enough* a qualifier of?

After some uncomfortable small talk about the weather, Connor waved to his park-issued vehicle. It was a big Cruiser, seven-seats, lots of storage. "We can load all your gear into the back," Connor said. "We can take one vehicle in on the fire trail, and it'll cut a good ten kilometres off our hike."

Well . . . well, maybe Connor wasn't so bad after all.

"This front is coming in by nightfall," Amy said, gesturing to the already-grey sky. "We need to be over the first bluff and have camp set up before dark or . . ."

"Or what?" I asked.

"Snow makes the ridge impassable."

Snow. Excellent.

Vince pulled out a map and he drew his finger along the path we'd be taking, from where we stood to where we'd drive to, then the hike. He showed us where we'd camp tonight and where we'd be hiking tomorrow morning to the cave site. It was an intense climb, a popular track with experienced hikers. Not in winter, obviously, because most hikers weren't idiots. At any other time of year, there'd be cars parked and people about, but not in weather as dismal as this. He then proceeded to explain the abseiling requirements.

Connor's team was entrusted to bring the abseiling equipment for all of us to minimise our carrying burden, and the way he and Vince checked off their gear list out loud did make me feel better about their competence. They took this seriously, and I was pleased about that.

The cave itself was two thirds of the way up a rock cliff face. It was easier to hike to the top and abseil down than it was to rock climb. The plan was to spend the night in the cave, then abseil all the way down to the bottom to complete the trip. The cliff had three tiers of ledges and there were anchors drilled into each section, making the descent three shorter drops instead of one longer one. I felt better about that.

I had done some abseiling before, at Jack's insistence. At first, I'd been horrified at the suggestion, but after he'd explained the science behind it—physics and force versus mass and gravity—I understood it and had no issue in taking that first step over the edge.

Since then, we'd done it quite a few times. It was exhilarating and, dare I say it, fun.

Connor pointed his finger guns at me. "Now you did say you've abseiled before, right?"

I looked at his still-gun fingers, then at his face, wondering why on earth he thought that was a good idea. "Yes."

Jack chuckled beside me. "Come on, let's get our gear and get moving."

It was just after eleven o'clock, and the grey clouds were already low, the wind was cold, and everything was damp already. And there was a likelihood of snow, in which we were supposed to camp out.

Jack popped the boot of our park-issued four-wheel drive, which wasn't anywhere near as big as Connor's, and I glanced back at where Connor, Vince, and Amy were moving gear around.

"I thought you said Connor was nice enough," I whispered.

Jack grinned and stuffed his beanie into his coat pocket. "Got your beanie?"

I held it up to show him before stuffing it into my pocket, then I pulled my bags closer. "I cannot think of one scenario where finger guns are an appropriate form of communication."

Jack laughed at that and heaved his backpack strap over his shoulder. "Which is the bag with your lab gear in it?"

I patted the bag I was holding. "He probably does white-water rafting."

Jack looked at me then. "Who?"

"Mr Finger Guns." I slung my backpack over my shoulder. "I may not be adept at reading social cues like you, but I'm not naïve enough to know that he thinks I'm a book nerd who won't last five minutes out here."

Jack stopped pulling the tent bag over. "Why do you care what he thinks?"

"Because he's your colleague." Which I thought would be obvious. "Usually when we go on expeditions, we meet . . . people like me and my colleagues. People who know me, or know of me, and what to expect. But these are your people. I want to make a good impression for you."

Jack glanced over at the others and made a face. "Well, I'm gonna let you in a little secret, dear husband. I don't give one fuck what they think of me. I could not care less. I care what *you* think of me. All I expect from them is professionalism, their local expertise and knowledge, *and* that they respect you as a lepidopterist. Don't get me wrong, I'm grateful he called and notified you of the butterflies. But if he, or any of them, say one word to you that isn't appropriate, I will set them straight."

"I can remind people of their manners," I reminded him. "I'm very capable."

Jack snorted. "Oh, believe me, I know. But I'm pretty sure Connor wouldn't understand the big words you use, and I didn't bring a thesaurus or the crayons to explain it to him."

That made me smile. "Not even Brennan uses crayons anymore."

Laughing, Jack handed my last bag to me, closed the boot, and locked the car. We loaded everything into the Cruiser, Jack and I climbed into the back with Amy, and we set off down the fire trail.

WHEN CONNOR SAID the drive would cut ten kilometres off the trip, I was grateful, yes. But the trail we were driving on was no more a road than it was a billygoat track. It was all rough ups and sharp downs and bumps and bellyswooping jolts.

I now understood why Connor got a bigger four-wheel drive than Jack. This was hardcore off-roading, though I didn't dare complain or even squeak, even though I wanted to several times.

It was foggy, misty, wet, and incredibly cold. The forest had closed in on all sides, the track barely recognisable in front of us. But Vince and Amy kept conversation with Jack, asking him about the regeneration progress after the bushfires and, of course, Jack could talk about his work, his park, all day long. I spent the trip trying to read over the information I had on the cave we were heading to and the photographs Connor had taken of the specimens he'd collected. I couldn't see much detail, granted, but it was enough to keep me looking. There were photos of the cave that defied belief, and I couldn't wait to see it for myself.

And soon enough, the track was too rough for me to read anything, and after an eternity of off-roading hell, it ended. Though the spot Connor had declared was the end of the road looked no different to the path we'd just driven, if I was being honest. But I could hear a river now, rushing and loud, and the sounds of the forest came to life.

We sorted our bags, fitted our backpacks, attached our helmets to said backpacks, and ensured everything was secure and even-weighted. Knowing getting to this location was difficult, I hadn't even brought most of my gear. I was bringing only the basics, given we had to carry our camping things as well.

When we were ready to set off, Connor declared the direction and said we'd find the hiking trail about forty metres through the thicket, and sure enough, we did.

I feared we'd be hiking through rainforest without a path, but the track was well-walked and the footing easier than I'd expected. We walked single file, Connor at the lead, then Jack, then me, then Amy and Vince. Every so often, without stopping, Connor would call out, "How's my team?"

And without fail, Vince and Amy would reply with some variation of "Good, boss" or "All square, boss," and I liked that.

Perhaps I needed to reassess my initial impression of

Connor. Though the finger guns would live in infamy of awful.

We kept a good pace and made good time. We stopped an hour in for a drink and energy bar break, finding some quartzite boulders to sit on. It was a semi-cleared area and I got the impression it was a popular hiking stop.

"We start the ascent from here on in," Connor explained. It had been a steady incline for the last hour, but apparently now we were about to climb. "Everyone feeling okay?"

He looked at everyone, but his gaze finished on me. "Yes, perfectly fine, thank you," I replied. If he was expecting me to complain or cry for wanting to return home, he would be sorely disappointed. I slipped on my backpack, then picked up Jack's and helped him into it.

"You guys have obviously done this before?" Amy asked.

Jack gave her his charming grin. "Once or twice."

"I didn't know butterfly research was so . . . hands-on," she added.

I knew she meant no offence, but still. Did she think a butterfly's natural habitat was a research lab? "Lawson's been all over the country in his career," Jack said. There was no malice in his voice, just stating a fact. "And actually, I've learned more about ecology and environmental impacts by traipsing all through the wilderness with him. It's really fascinating."

Amy smiled. "I bet it is. And you've saved how many species from the brink of extinction?"

"Oh, um," I replied. "Well, I didn't save them single-handedly—"

Jack laughed. "Yes, he did. His modesty belies the truth."

"A lot of my time is spent in my research lab," I said, ignoring Jack's boasting. "But to observe a specimen in their natural habitat is very important. There is a direct correlation between the species' health and the habitat in which we find them."

"And you built your own butterfly house?" Vince joined in. "I read about it when Connor said you were coming here."

I gave a nod. "Yes. Jack built it for me. It's amazing."

"Will you take some of these species back to your butterfly house?" Amy asked.

"That depends on a few factors, and I won't know until I see them," I replied. I rather liked that Vince and Amy were excited about this expedition. "Should we keep moving?"

"Yep," Connor said, and we began on the path again.

Up and up the path went. He wasn't kidding when he said the ascent started. It didn't seem to ever stop. But onward we went, never complaining, never stopping. Rocks and tree roots made a natural staircase for the most part, and my thighs and lungs were starting to burn. But we trod carefully and Connor asked every so often how his team was travelling.

Then the trees and forest suddenly thinned out, and we simply appeared to climb out of the forest and into shrubland that hunkered down from the wind. The entire side of the mountain was low brush and grasses and sheets of ancient quartzite we had to clamber up.

The wind was biting now and it was hard to tell if it was sleeting or biting rain. I couldn't see how high up we were as we were fully immersed in mist, or cloud, for all I knew. I had my beanie and gloves on and was thankful for the weatherproof outerwear that Jack insisted we buy for our Snowy Mountains trip a few years ago.

And we trudged onward and upward further still. Until we stopped again at a wall of craggy rock that provided a bit of a windbreak. And, pridefully, I was pleased to see I wasn't the only one out of breath.

We all were.

"We're almost there," Connor said, his cheeks flushed. "We cross the bluff, then we set up camp for the night."

Everyone nodded and sipped their waters and gluco-gels. It was three o'clock, and it'd be dark by five. Jack gave me a look with a smile that asked me if I was okay without saying a word. I gave a slight nod and he returned the gesture. I took my phone from my thigh pocket and began taking photographs of the flora interspersed between the grey rock formations that now dominated this landscape. Trying to record much else was futile with the mist.

"I wish you could see the view," Connor said, nodding out into the grey cloud that surrounded us. "It's amazing. Fingers crossed the cloud's lifted by tomorrow. You can see near all the way to the west coast."

I took barometric readings and could only shake my head. "And the photographs you sent me were taken this week?"

Connor gave half a shrug and nod. "Sure. Is that unusual?"

I wanted to laugh at that, but it wasn't his fault he didn't know. "Extremely. Butterflies are dormant during winter. Especially at this elevation, given the rainforest below us would typically be an ideal habitat. I'm yet to see inside the cave, obviously. But these readings," I held up the barome-ter. "To say it's unusual to find a colony of active butterflies in these conditions would be an understatement."

Jack's smile was breathtaking. "This is exciting."

I nodded, smiling right back at him. "It could be, yes. Very."

Amy clapped her hands together, the exhilaration tangible. "Then let's keep moving."

Getting to the bluff itself was steep. We basically had to use narrow-formed footholds while climbing up the rocks, sometimes heaving ourselves up. Connor had called them natural steps, but I had to wonder which giant he was referring to.

By the time I'd pulled myself up the last step, I was fast approaching done. Everyone was puffing and panting, so thankfully it wasn't just me. But I was glad the top of the bluff was relatively flat, though the wind was a hundred ice needles into my face. The mist was dense now, so I could barely see a few metres in any direction. The patches of grass and rock were slippery, and while it was tempting to hunker down and run to get out of the wind, treading slow and sure was safer.

A twisted ankle or broken leg up here was a helicopter ride out, and no helicopter was landing in this weather.

We crossed the bluff and made our way down a rocky escarpment and found ourselves on a grassy area that was blocked from the wind by a rock face. Connor took off his backpack and grinned at us. "We set up here tonight."

"Oh my word, that's so much better," I said as I shrugged out of my backpack.

Jack did the same and put his hand on my arm. His cheeks were pink and he was puffing out steam. "Remind you of anything?"

I chuckled. "I was only just thinking about how an ankle or leg injury would be a disaster up here."

"Don't jinx us," Vince said, dropping his backside onto the ground. He was puffing hard.

"I wouldn't be piggybacking you down this mountain," Jack said, taking a sip of water. "The Snowy Mountains incident was . . . character building." Then, much to my dismay, he explained for the others. "Lawson twisted his ankle on an expedition on Kosciuszko."

"On the bright side," I said, aiming for funny, "at least there are no cane toads or inland taipans here."

Jack laughed. "There are tiger snakes in these parts."

"Oh good."

"But they're all be hibernating right now," Amy said.

"I've heard that before," I mumbled.

Jack chuckled. "Inland taipan bites are not recommended."

I shook my head. "Neither is cane toad toxin."

The three of them stared at us, wide-eyed. "Are you two cursed or something?" Connor asked.

I snorted. "Not at all. We've been on dozens of expeditions together. Our near-fatal incident rate is well below ten per cent."

"Oh good," Vince deadpanned. "Ten per cent."

Jack laughed. "What good is almost dying if not to remind us we're alive?"

Amy smiled at that. "I love that you two go on these adventures together. It is honestly relationship goals."

I sipped my water and wiped my mouth. "It has its perks," I said. "Like when my husband says he'll put the tent up and start dinner while I go over my notes."

Jack laughed again. "Or when your husband does his share and stops being lazy."

I sighed and tried not to smile. Jack unclipped the

rolled-up tent and threw it near my feet. "It was worth a try."

We were fast running out of daylight, so we all did our tents first. They each had those single pop-up tents, which made sense. But Jack and I had a two-man style. Well, it fit two men . . . if they didn't mind getting cosy with each other, which luckily we didn't. We rolled out our sleeping bags, which I promptly unzipped and rezipped up as one larger sleeping bag for two men who didn't mind getting cosy with each other.

Jack smiled and waggled his eyebrow at me. "Don't get any ideas, Mr Brighton-Gale," I whispered. We were in our tent and it wasn't as though they could see us or hear us. "We'll be warmer if we share a sleeping bag. I'm far too tired and sore for anything else."

He chuckled, that throaty and warm sound I loved so much. "To be honest, Mr Brighton-Gale, I'm more excited just to camp out with you. We should do this more often."

"Camping, yes. Hiking, maybe not."

"It wasn't an easy one, was it?"

I shook my head and spoke to ensure the others would definitely not hear. "Not that I'd ever admit it to them, but I was very glad to stop tonight."

Jack kissed me quickly. "Same. And Lawson, don't feel like you're not on par with them, because you are. You hiked and climbed like a pro today."

"We still have the abseiling tomorrow to get through."

"And we'll nail it." Jack was so sure of it, and I wished for his confidence. "Don't worry about that right now, and think about the butterflies you're going to see tomorrow. I'll make us some dinner."

CHAPTER THREE

JACK

AFTER DINNER, everyone was eager for sleep. It had been a long day: a pretty gruelling hike after a four-hour car drive. Connor had run through a few safety specs for where we were camping. "If you get up for a midnight pee, don't go too far. We're fairly secure here, but if you wander off too far in the dark, there's a helluva drop. Hope no one sleep-walks." Then he stopped and stared. "No, seriously, does anyone here sleepwalk?"

Vince and Amy both laughed and said no, and of course Lawson and I would be fine. There was no way I was letting Lawson wander off by himself in the dark when we were camped on the side of a mountain.

But we all bid each other a good night, said we would see each other at six o'clock. I doubted there'd be any need for alarms . . . I had to wonder how much sleep we'd be getting.

Lawson and I zipped up the tent, took our boots off, and climbed into our sleeping bag. It was freezing cold. All of 2°C and a wind chill factor of -9°C. The ground was cold but Lawson snuggled himself right into me, and I wrapped him up tight and sighed.

"I wonder what Brennan's doing," he murmured.

"He'd be reading a book with Grandma. Already bathed and in his jarmies, he'd have had his dinner, and I think Aunty Poppy will be making hot chocolates right about now."

He sighed. "I miss him."

"Me too." I held him a little bit tighter. "But I love being here with you too."

"Same." He stretched, then groaned. "My legs hurt."

I chuckled. "Mine too."

"Can't wait to see these butterflies tomorrow. They better still be there."

I rubbed his back and kissed the side of his head. "I'm sure they will be. After all, they're waiting for you to find them."

He let out a happy sigh and he drifted off to sleep. I tried to fight the weight of my eyelids, the ache in my legs and my back, but the day beat me. With Lawson safe and warm in my arms, I drifted off to sleep.

The howling wind woke me up around midnight, pulling at the tent and trying to fling us off the mountain. Then all of a sudden the wind was gone, replaced by a gentle pattering sound on the roof of the tent. It took me a moment to realise what it was.

It was snowing.

I smiled into the darkness and pulled Lawson against me. He mumbled something that sounded mostly like my name, but he never woke.

I hoped the snow didn't impede the final leg of our trip. Inclement weather would often close walking tracks in national parks, but we weren't the public. We weren't some public liability risk. We were national park employees on a work-related trip. We did this kind of thing all the time.

Plus, Lawson would be devastated to come this far and not be able to take the final step.

Knowing only time would tell if this expedition was over, I closed my eyes and hoped for a few more hours of sleep before we found out.

THE SOUND of a zipper woke me up, followed by the trudge of footsteps as one of the other three got up, presumably to go pee.

"What time is it?" Lawson mumbled.

I lifted my hand and peered at my watch in the dark. The sky was beginning to lighten but only barely. "Five thirty," I replied. I tried to stretch out a bit to test my muscles. "I'm not as sore as I thought I'd be."

"Hmm." He stretched his legs and rolled his shoulders. "Same." He sat up and scrubbed his hands over his face and let out a bit of a groan. "Though my back says hello."

I chuckled, but then I remembered last night. "I think it snowed during the night."

Lawson sat still for a second until it seemed he remembered what that could mean for our expedition, and then he was climbing out of the sleeping bad. "Come on. Let's take a look at the damage."

The damage was a light dusting of fine white snow and clumps of build-up driven by the wind around tufts of grass and rocks. It was a cold -4°C on the thermometer, but the wind was, at the moment, thankfully, gone.

The mist was absent too, leaving behind an amazing view. Behind us, to the northeast, was a valley of forest and, further out, farmland, as far as the eye could see. The sun was just beginning to make its mark on the horizon with a light show of blues and pinks and yellows across the entire valley, and honestly, it was one hell of an impressive view to wake up to.

I stood there, not quite believing how pretty it was. "Wow."

"It's gorgeous, isn't it?" Amy said, walking back into camp. It must have been her we'd heard earlier.

"What do we make of the snow?" Lawson asked. "Enough to call a stop to our trip?"

She looked around at the snow and made a face. "Honestly, hard to tell. We'll wait until Connor makes a decision and how long we can put it off. We might just have to hold leaving off for an hour or so, but I'm just guessing."

Within a few minutes, both Connor and Vince were up and out of their tents. Connor wasn't happy about the snow, or maybe disappointed was more the case. But after breakfast, it was decided that Connor, Vince, and I would walk on and scout out the area. If it was too dangerous, there'd be no abseiling, and that was a decision I respected.

How long we'd wait it out for, though, would be the true test of patience for Lawson.

Leaving Amy and Lawson to pack everything up—and hopefully keep him busy and distracted enough—Connor, Vince, and I climbed up the rockface and trod our way to the edge of the cliff. There were a few clumps of snow but not as much as I thought there would be.

The view was . . . oh my god, it was beautiful. Connor had been right. We could almost see the west coast from the top. The hike, the difficulty, the aching muscles were worth it for the view alone. It almost looked like something from a movie. Obviously an extinct volcano, the rocky edges formed a somewhat-circular basin which was now a lake and rainforest.

I took out my phone and snapped some photos. "Wow."

Connor grinned. "Nice, huh?"

"Stunning."

"Never gets old," Vince said.

"What's your assessment?" Connor asked him.

Vince looked around, scraping his boots on the rock, and he peered down over the edge. Then he went to one point of the rock we stood on and scraped away clumps of snow to reveal a row of u-bolts drilled into the rock. He inspected them thoroughly. "Anchors look good. There's no surface ice, it's just powdery, and the sun'll make short work of that." He stood up and met Connor's gaze. "I think we're good to go."

I grinned. "That's gonna make someone very happy."

Vince's smile matched mine. "Do you reckon they've finished packing everything up yet, or should we give them a few minutes?"

Connor snorted and shook his head. "Get your arse back down there and help."

He laughed and began the walk back to camp, and Connor rolled his eyes. "Kids, huh? If he wasn't an expert climber . . ."

"I heard that," Vince called out without turning around.

I chuckled as we made our way back, and Lawson had the tent put away and was staring at Vince. Then when he saw me, he rushed over. "Well, what's the verdict? Vince wouldn't say."

"I wasn't giving the news," Vince said, trying not to smile.

Lawson was bordering on panic, and I could see the

disappointment creeping into his eyes. Until I smiled. "Get ready to find your butterflies. We are a go."

Lawson beamed, then shot Vince a foul look. "You made me worry."

Vince laughed. "Let's finish here and run through our safety specs and descent details, yeah?"

I rubbed Lawson's back. "You wait till you see the view."

"Amy, have we got a weather update?" Connor asked.

Amy read directly from her device screen. "Light southerly, three knots, tops. Temps today to reach twelve degrees, clear skies."

"And tomorrow?"

"Storms expected to roll in around noon. We'll need to be down the mountain by the time that hits."

Connor looked directly at Lawson. "You have all of today and tonight to collect whatever you need, but we're abseiling out of there tomorrow morning after breakfast. No questions."

Lawson gave him a nod. "Understood."

Vince had pulled out a large folded map of the cliff face with black lines drawn down it, and he proceeded to tell us how this would happen.

The mouth of the cave, eighteen metres down, had an excellent landing ledge.

Connor would descend first, then Lawson, then me, then all our gear, then Amy, and Vince would watch anchor and be the last to come down. Tonight would be spent inside the cave, and tomorrow morning we'd take the same order down to the two ledges as we made our way down to the bottom.

This wasn't a difficult abseil. All abseiling was dangerous, granted, but in the warmer months, people made this descent every other week. It was listed as intermediate. The lack of wind was good and there were no overhangs. Vince had done much harder as a child, he'd boasted. But still . . . all abseiling was dangerous.

When we got everything packed away and made our way up to the top, the rising sun made the view even better. "How are you feeling?" I asked Lawson quietly.

He knew I wasn't questioning the decision to do this or his ability. I was simply asking if he was in the right mind-set. Yes, he was excited and eager to get down into that cave, but one wrong move and this could all end very badly. "Good, and you?"

"I'm good. This is going to be great."

He gave me a hard nod, his gaze focused and serious. "I'm ready."

CHAPTER FOUR

LAWSON

WATCHING Connor step over the edge put my stomach through the wringer. Vince, albeit young, was very good at what he did. If I'd thought him to be frivolous and rambunctious—and I could admit that I had—then I was wrong.

He'd been rock climbing and abseiling since he could walk, apparently. And admittedly, I felt much better knowing he was in charge of the ropes and anchor.

I'd discerned that Vince was the wild one, Amy was the science one, and Connor was the older brother who kept everything in line. Together, the three of them made a pretty good team.

When Connor was safely down and it was my turn, Vince and Jack helped me into the harness and triple-checked everything. But when it came time to step backwards over the edge, my feet were literally on the precipice, Jack stood too close to me. Worry etched his features, and he looked a little pale.

"Please move back," I told him.

Jack blinked. "I'm two metres from the edge. I have a safety harness."

"Jack, I'm not joking," I said, firmer this time. "Please step back from the edge."

Vince tried not to smile, Amy just grinned away, but Jack refused to step back. "Be careful. Watch your footing," he said.

"I've done this before, you'll remember."

"Lawson." Jack's tone was sharp. "Focus and concentrate."

"Mm," Amy said. "Maybe it's not relationship goals to do this with your partner."

I pursed my lips and stepped out backwards, meeting Jack's eyes. "See you down there. Don't be late."

He smiled then, and step by slow-and-steady step, I descended. I daren't look out at the vastness of open air behind me, and I certainly didn't look down. I kept my breathing even, concentrated on where my feet and hands were at all times, keeping each movement steady. I was relieved and surprised when Connor's voice got closer, and then he was directing me down to the ledge and then beside me and holding me steady.

I unhooked myself free, with adrenaline-shaking hands and knees, and quickly made my way into the mouth of the cave. With terra firma under my feet, I could breathe a bit easier.

But I'd breathe a whole lot easier when Jack was with me.

Connor talked him through it, like he did with me, and as soon as his legs appeared, I was ready to grab him until he had two feet on the ledge. We got him out of the rigging, and I pulled him in for a hug.

"You okay?" he asked, his arms wrapped tight around me.

"Better now," I replied.

He kissed the side of my head. "It's as easy as stepping off a mountain."

I laughed then, just as Connor said, "Here's the first of the gear."

We unhooked the bags and I set them down to one side, out of the way. I could see enough of the front of the cave. The mouth itself was perhaps four metres tall by three metres wide, but inside it opened up like a room. But without lighting, I couldn't see much more than jagged rock walls and dirt for a floor.

More gear came down next and I put it to one side. I found my bag and pulled out a lamp, switching it on, amazed at what it revealed.

We seemed to be in a first chamber, some ten-metres wide by ten- or twelve-metres long. The ceiling was uneven and jagged rock probably five-metres high. And it was, for all intents and purposes, empty.

There was a fissure in the rock wall toward the back of the chamber, like a narrow doorway. I would imagine that led to the other two parts of the cave, and that was where I needed to go—I told myself to be patient. The last of the gear came down, then Amy followed, and Jack and Connor helped get her down. She looked as relieved as I felt, and I patted her shoulder when she came over.

"Solid rock never felt so good," I said.

She grinned. "God, yes." Then she looked around. "Oh wow."

"Amazing, yes?" I shone the torch toward the fissure. "There's a doorway through there, to the other two chambers, I would think."

She nodded and already had her barometer reader out. "This is so cool."

It was warmer inside the cave, and if it was warmer for

us, that meant it would be warmer for other creatures too. Namely butterflies, but also . . . "Uh, will there be snakes in here?"

Jack and Connor were helping Vince plant his feet on the ledge, so my question fell to Amy. "Uh, I don't think so," she replied. "I mean, I can't guarantee there won't be. But the rainforest below is warmer, and that's where the birds' eggs, frogs, and rats are. I can't imagine there's be much for a snake to eat up here."

Sounded reasonable, and we could hope.

Vince came in, holding his ropes and gear, grinning. "Starting without me?"

"Thank you," I answered. "Your expertise in rappelling is most appreciated."

He grinned some more, as though what I'd said was funny. "No worries. You handled it like a pro."

"Made easier by your confidence and assurance," I added, the compliment most deserving in my opinion. But Vince cast me an odd look as though I was making fun of him.

Jack chuckled and clapped Vince on the shoulder. "You did good." Then he turned back to the entrance. "Look at that view."

The mouth of the cave now framed the most spectacular landscape picture nature could probably provide. And truth be told, I could appreciate it more from here than I did at the very top. It felt like we were on top of the world.

"And there are just the three chambers?" I asked.

"Yep." Connor nodded toward the end of the cave. "There's no secret passages or channels, just three large rooms, much like this one. The third one is a bit smaller."

"And are there other caves in this mountain range?"

"Uh, yes. Several. None this high up though," Connor

replied. He gestured to the rock wall. "This is quartzite and limestone, some seven-hundred-million years old. Last time that volcano probably erupted would have taken out some dinosaurs, but it left some remarkable formations."

I nodded, my interest piqued. If the cave played a part in the required ecosystem for this butterfly, we could have several locations to inspect. I turned toward the fissure at the end of the first chamber. "Well . . . shall we?"

"Hell yes," Jack said. "Let's just look first, worry about the scientific stuff second."

I rolled my eyes, not even mad. His excitement about finding butterflies made my heart so happy. I lifted my torch. "Okay then, let's go. Now the butterflies were in the third chamber, right?"

Amy nodded. "Yep."

So I walked first, Jack close behind me, and we passed through the split in the rockface into the second chamber. It was so dark, and my torch lit a halo of light around us, but I'd hate to think of being in here without it.

The second chamber was roughly the same size as the first, though it sloped downward at the end of the long room. The ceiling was rougher and darker though, and . . . did it just move?

"Um," I whispered, staring up.

Then, like something out of a nightmare, the entire ceiling rushed toward us—and toward the only escape—in a swarm of screeching bats.

Jack grabbed hold of me with a sharp intake of breath; Amy let out a startled scream. Or maybe it was Connor. I couldn't tell. Not that I could blame them . . .

"Bats," I breathed, shaking off the residual heebie-jeebies.

Amy still had her hands over her head, ducking down

low, and Connor looked three shades of white. Vince just chuckled. "Southern forest bat," he said.

I held the light up again and there were still a few bats clinging to the ceiling that seemed content to stay, and I was happy to leave them.

This chamber definitely sloped downward and the crevice-like opening at the far end seemed to go down deeper still. The temperature dropped the further in we went and we scanned the craggy floor for snakes and thankfully found none. It was probably too cold for them. Though there were a few bugs and scurrying whispers, the cave floor was mostly critter-free. The critters hanging from the ceiling were fine . . . as long as they stayed on the ceiling.

The entrance into the third chamber was narrow and long, downward-sloping and cold, and a little slippery. But soon enough the passage opened up into a very dark and dank room. We scanned the floor area first for any potential danger. There were sharp rock formations, some of the walls were jagged, some were smooth, but it was thankfully minus snakes.

Then I scanned up to the ceiling.

I'd seen photos, but what I saw took my breath away.

An entire kaleidoscope of butterflies hung from the ceiling. A pink kaleidoscope.

There in the dark of a remote cave, halfway up a cliff face, was an entire colony of butterflies I'd never seen before.

Pink.

In the dark. In winter.

It was mind-boggling.

I put my hand to my mouth and blinked back tears. I glanced to Jack to find him staring upward with a huge grin, and when he felt my eyes on him, he turned to me. "Lawson . . ."

I nodded, not trusting my voice to speak.

"So, Doc," Connor said. "Whaddya think? Is it a new species?"

I swallowed hard and tried to settle my nerves, my excitement. "I'll need to examine and study . . ." I trailed off. He didn't know, nor care, about the process. "But, yes. I do believe we might be looking at a new species."

The three of them all grinned, excited and probably relieved. There had been a good chance that we'd have come all this way for nothing.

But Jack's smile was something else. There was so much love, pride, and happiness there. He put his hand to my shoulder and pulled me in for a hug. He was all warmth and sweat, and being in his arms was my one true happy place. But this wasn't really the time for that.

"Uh, Jack," I mumbled. "You're squashing the light."

"Oh, sorry." He pushed me back to arms-length. "Okay, so let's get started. We need a grid set up, torch in every corner. Do not step on any casings or . . . actually, just stick to the walls as close as you can. Don't walk underneath them, no direct light on them, no loud noises—"

"Uh, Jack. Thanks, but I can handle this," I said. Well, I would have had it, but now it was too late. I turned to the other three. "Okay, well, what Jack said is fine."

And so the real work began.

I took a myriad of readings, images, footage, and some fallen, expired casings and already-dead specimens from the cave floor.

Vince and Connor eventually left us to it, choosing to spend their time in the first chamber, which was probably for the best. Where we were was an enclosed space and I'd eliminated most of the floor space, so room was limited. But Amy stayed, thrilled at every turn. Most would find the work boring and tedious, but she loved the data collation. She monitored humidity, temperatures, and she was fastidious in her work. Everything was neat and precise, and I was duly impressed.

"What kind of lichen is that?" she asked.

The ceiling had a rivulet of water, filtered by a few hundred thousand tonnes of rock that fed a patch of moss-like lichen that clung to the ceiling like a carpet.

"It looks like a pink or purple lichen," Jack said frowning. "We're going to need a sample of that."

I turned to him. "What do you mean a pink or purple lichen? Usually you speak in botanical names."

He smirked and shrugged. "I'm not familiar with it."

"You're not . . ." I blinked, trying to piece his words together. "You're never not familiar with a plant type."

He pointed upward. "That resembles something like the *Cryptohecia rubrocinta* or the *Arthoniaceae*, which is a lichenised type of fungus." Then he looked at me. "But neither of those should be here. Not in a cave, not at these temperatures, and not in Australia. I mean, we have some lichens that are close, but not like that."

I blinked again and felt a little light-headed, if I was being honest. "A new species?"

"I can't say. Not until we've taken samples for analysis." He looked back up at the ceiling. "Could it explain the colour of the butterflies?"

"You think there's a dietary pigmentation transference?"

Jack shrugged. "Honestly, I have no clue."

I thought about that for a moment. "It would make sense. Similar to a flamingo, per se. I don't like the chances of a coincidence. Pink lichen produces pink butterflies." It was all so much to think about. Two new species found together?

Then Amy, who had been quiet all through this, said, "What are the odds of the lichen changing colour because of *its* diet?" She looked at each of us in turn. "Flamingos are pink because of the carotenoids in shrimp, right? Like you said. But in the plant world, it's like the hydrangea. Too much aluminium in the soil, you have blue flowers. If you want to turn them pink, add lime." She then looked up to the ceiling of the cave. "Not much of a stretch to presume that water trickle runs through limestone. Perhaps this lichen is similar to the hydrangea?"

I grinned at her. "Deductive reasoning. I like it."

"I like it too," Jack said. "We'll know more when we can get it analysed."

"And to find butterflies in winter is not common?" Amy asked as she took more readings. "I know Connor said it was odd."

"Caterpillars usually spend colder months as eggs or larvae, even pupa," I explained. "They have an internal thermometer, of sorts, called diapause. It's found all through nature, including mammals. It tells them when to hibernate or migrate in winter and when to mate for spring. Butter-flies will usually migrate. Overwintering will see a decline in egg production . . ." I stopped myself from going on and on about it. "To answer your question, finding butterflies in the imago phase, which is active sexual maturity in this case, at these temperatures and in complete darkness, is rare. Possibly unique." I added another dead specimen to my collection. "Normally, butterflies prefer temperatures above ten or twelve degrees to fly and function. What temperature do we have now?"

Amy read off her screen. "It's five-point-three degrees."

"And being wet and cold usually kills butterflies," Jack added. "The lichen provides a food source and a water source but acts as a sponge for them. So they can drink without getting wet."

"Even lichen as a primary food source is rare," I pointed out. "Caterpillars and moths can live on lichen, and there is one type of butterfly in Sri Lanka I'm aware of which prefers it. And to be honest, this butterfly shares some behavioural characteristics of the moth. But the lichen food source is an odd symbiotic relationship. Lichens accumulate large concentrations of secondary metabolites, like aromatic phenolic compounds, such as atranorin and usnic acid." I glanced over at Jack. "It must deter the bats from eating them." I shook my head in wonder. "How remarkable."

"Can I ask a really obvious question?" Amy asked. "You'll probably think I'm stupid."

"No I won't," I replied. No question in the quest for education was stupid.

She made a face. "What's the difference between a moth and butterfly? I mean, except the fact that moths are usually brown and butterflies are all kinds of colours. And that we see butterflies during the day but see moths at night."

I smiled. "You almost answered your own question. There is a colour differential. Butterflies typically have more colouring. Butterflies are diurnal, moths are nocturnal. But there are other differences. The way they fold their wings in a resting position is probably the most obvious, but also the antennae are different and the frenulum."

She blinked. "I'm sorry, the what?"

Jack laughed. "Not that kind. This is a different kind. In insects."

I caught on to what she meant. "Oh." Dear God, I hoped she couldn't see the flame of my cheeks. "Heavens no. Uh, moths have a wing-coupling for flight that butterflies do not have. Also, the butterfly pupa is made from hardened protein; the moth pupa is spun from silk. The casings here in this cave are not silk."

I held up the dead specimen in my jar, inspecting it as best I could with the poor light. "But these eyes are . . ."

Jack walked over to me. "They're what?"

I took a deep breath and exhaled slowly, not really believing it myself. "I want to get a better look in my lab, but I might have a theory."

"You noticed something," he prompted.

"I can't say with any certainty yet, and I may be jumping to conclusions."

"What is it?"

"Ask me how I know this species has never been documented before."

"Christ, Lawson, just say it."

I smiled at him. "This species is almost certainly a butterfly. The thorax, the scaling, the wings, antennae are all butterfly. But the eyes . . ."

"The eyes are what?"

"This species has superposition eyes. Butterflies do not have superposition eyes, they have apposition eyes. Moths have superposition eyes because they're nocturnal; the eye reflects light differently."

Jack's brow quirked upward. "And you've never heard of a butterfly with the eyes of a moth."

I grinned. "Never."

"So is this a new species of butterfly?" Amy asked. "Or a whole new species?"

I chewed on my lip and looked again to the specimen in my jar, trying not to smile. "I can't say with certainty."

"Holy shit," Jack said. "It is. It's a whole new *specimen*. Because if you've never heard of it, it doesn't exist."

"Well, it may have existed a long time ago," I interjected, trying not to sound too hopeful. "Perhaps it was lost a few hundred years ago and we've only just *rediscovered* it. I'll need to do a lot of research. And there is much we don't know. Do they spend their entire lifecycles inside this cave? Do they see daylight at all? What is their lifecycle? Have they simply evolved over thousands of years to adapt to the dark? Many troglofaunal species do this."

"Troglofaunal?" Amy repeated.

"Cave-dwelling animals."

"Well," Jack said regardless of my information dump. "It's exciting nonetheless."

"It is," I agreed. "I think we can leave them be for the time being. I don't want the light to upset them any more than we need to. Let's pack up and go out to the others."

I had no idea what the time was, given the inside of the cave was impervious to day or night.

"Though I would like to try one thing," I added after we'd packed up our gear and were just about to walk out. I took one live specimen, held it very carefully, and we made our way back out through the chambers toward the daylight.

Then, standing in the middle of the first chamber, with daylight still streaming in, I opened the jar. The butterfly crawled up out of the plastic specimen container, tasting the air with its proboscis. I wanted to see if it was drawn to the daylight, but it took off, flittering through the air toward the back of the cave, through the fissure, and disappeared back into the darkness.

All I could do was shake my head. "Remarkable."

CHAPTER FIVE

JACK

THIS WAS GROUND-BREAKING STUFF. And I'd seen Lawson discover new butterflies before. I'd seen his face, his smile, the light of wonder in his eyes.

But this wasn't just a new butterfly.

This was a new species. A butterfly-moth cross. A sub-species? A new lepidopteran classification? A new species entirely?

And to see Lawson discover this, to be part of the team that discovered this, was an extraordinary thing.

He got the same look in his eyes when he watched Brennan. When Brennan took his first step, said "daddy" for the first time.

That was the look Lawson got when he realised he was seeing something utterly wondrous.

It did things to my heart I wasn't quite prepared for.

"Pretty special, huh?" Amy asked me quietly. We were taking soil samples from the second chamber, and Lawson was spending time with the butterflies, recording their behaviour patterns.

I realised I was smiling at Amy like a crazy man. "It's pretty special, yeah."

"You're very lucky," she whispered, "to get to work with your husband."

There was something wistful, or wishful, about how she said that. I tried to piece it together. I nodded toward the first chamber. "Do you . . . are you and Vince or Connor . . . ?"

She looked aghast. "Oh, no!"

"Oh, sorry. I just wondered if you meant . . . you've mentioned relationship goals a few times, and I thought . . ."

She chewed on the inside of her lip for a second. "My partner," she whispered. "Works for a Tassie Devil conservation group. To work with her every day would be . . . amazing."

To work with *her* . . .

Oh.

She'd just divulged something incredibly personal to me, and I wasn't quite sure what to do with it. She swallowed hard. "It's just that I see you and your husband doing this . . ."

I reached over and gave Amy's arm a squeeze. "Don't let anyone tell you no or that you can't."

She nodded quickly, relieved and a little emotional. "One day we might get to make it happen."

I finished writing on the label of a sample of bat droppings. "You know, it takes a special kind of tenacity to make it happen. And that guy in there," I said, pointing my pen toward the third chamber where Lawson was. "He's the brave one out of us two. He never gives up, and years ago, he told his boss at the university how it was going to happen and how he was in charge and how he would be moving to

Tasmania to pursue the butterfly he found. His thesis was also basically an open letter to the butterfly association to tell them they were a bunch of idiots." I chuckled at that. "Which was before I even knew him. But he was right. Add in the fact that he's a genius, it's kinda hard to argue with anything he says because he's right almost all of the time. But he's stubborn and he knows what he wants, and he wanted to involve me with his work, and it's been incredible. Not just to be part of it and to experience it myself, but to see *him* experience it."

God, I was off-track.

"So, Amy," I added. "If you want to work with your girl, you find a way and you make it happen. Be the tenacious one. Don't let the boys-club attitude dictate anything."

She smiled and tucked a strand of hair behind her ear. "Sounds like a dream."

"You know," I said. "Lawson saved two devil joeys from certain death. He almost died doing it, by the way. And then I almost died hauling his arse out of there. But . . ." I was getting off-track again. "We have a listed colony of devils in my park, up north. If your partner wanted to apply through my office to come and observe them, I'm sure I could make that happen. And it is protocol to have someone from the national park assist them, which you could also apply for, through my office. Because if someone from my office can't attend, then I'm sure someone from a different national park, such as yourself, could step in."

Her smile became a grin. "Are you serious?"

I chuckled. "Absolutely." I packed away my gear. "You've proved yourself here. I know you're capable, and I know Lawson's impressed with your work."

"He is?"

"Sure he is."

"How do you know?"

"Because he hasn't asked you *not* to touch anything. If he didn't think you were capable, he'd have told you to sit with the others and not touch anything. In fact, he's trusted you with *his* work, and he doesn't trust anyone who isn't great at their job. And I'll let you in on a little secret," I whispered. "He's not impressed by many people."

I could see the blush on her cheeks, even in the darkened cave. She smiled at me. "I'm very honoured."

I looked up at the bats. "How about we get out of here. I don't want to get peed on."

"Good idea."

We took all our samples and gear back into the first chamber and packed it all away; then I was about to go check on Lawson, but he walked out holding his laptop. He propped it up on one of the bags and opened the screen. "The night vision camera is all set up," he explained. "I'd rather not disturb them any more than we have. Hopefully they'll settle down now and return to normal behaviour, and hopefully the night camera will return some good footage."

"That'll record all night?" Connor asked.

Lawson gave a nod. "I'd like to get one set up on a more permanent basis, but that's something we can discuss later. If this proves to be what I think it might."

"And you think it's a new species?" Vince repeated. "Not just a new species of butterfly."

Lawson smiled. "It's a strong possibility. And I'm afraid of what that might mean for your national park, your team, and how busy this might get for you. This is going to create quite the buzz."

"So we can expect to make this trip quite a bit," Connor deduced.

Lawson shrugged. "Well, Vince perhaps."

Connor blinked back his surprise. "Oh."

Lawson made a face. "Given his rappelling expertise." Then he looked to me and made another face. "Not for any other reason."

All I could do was laugh because the idea of Lawson wanting to spend time with Vince by choice was just funny. "I think we'll be back a fair bit." I looked to everyone in turn, still smiling. "How about we think about dinner?"

LAWSON KEPT an eye on his laptop screen, and he took one last temperature recording, but soon enough it was late enough and cold enough to crawl into bed.

We still set up our tents inside the first chamber of the cave. They gave an added layer of insulation for warmth, and they gave me and Lawson some privacy.

Once the door was zipped, we brushed our teeth the best we could, pulled off our boots, and climbed into our double sleeping bag. It had been a pretty incredible day, and I had to wonder how much sleep Lawson would be getting tonight. I was one hundred per cent certain he'd be up every hour looking at that night vision screen, watching, tracking, and reporting on the butterflies.

"I'm cold," he mumbled, snuggling into me.

I pulled him closer and rubbed his back. "Is that better?"

He snuggled in some more. "No. Still cold."

For a brief moment, I wondered if he was beginning to feel unwell, but then he ran his hand down to my hip and gripped the waistband of my pants. "Still cold," he said again, pulling me closer. "Would be a lot warmer with your body weight on mine."

I chuckled but obliged. I would always oblige him. It

took a bit of manoeuvring, all while trying to be quiet, and Lawson opened his legs as wide as the sleeping bag would allow.

Right, then.

"Lawson," I murmured. "There are others close by. They might hear."

"Hear what?" he whispered. It was dark, but with our noses touching, I could see his eyes. "I wouldn't be so bold as to suggest anything that might make noise, Jack. But you could kiss me. You could kiss me for hours."

I ghosted a kiss over his lips. "Promise you'll be quiet?"

He smiled, victorious and daring. "Can you?"

I kissed him then, like I owned him, like he was mine to do with whatever I wanted. I slid my arms underneath him and held him, devouring his mouth and sucking on his tongue. I could feel it in his body when he surrendered to it. He relaxed and welcomed it, and he groaned low in his throat.

I pulled back abruptly. "Quiet, or I'll stop."

It took his eyes a second to focus, and then he shook his head. "More."

Mmm, this Lawson was my favourite. The uninhibited, lost-to-the-pleasure Lawson who had no idea how sexy he was.

If we were home, I'd have him undressed and be buried inside him right now. And god, how I wanted to be.

But we weren't at home.

So I took a second to cool it, despite how hard we both were, and I just enjoyed it for what it was. We weren't going to get off, there would be no mind-blowing orgasm. We could just enjoy a make-out session instead.

We hadn't just made-out in so long. Since Brennan came into our lives, basically. Our daddy time was spent getting from point a to z in the most efficient ways possible. Which was fine. It's what most new parents did. But now we had some time to enjoy all those letters in after the a without getting to the z.

There was such intimacy in just kissing, in holding each other, in nuzzling necks, and more kissing. Soft kissing, deep kissing, tender and hard, tasting and biting, with no intention of taking it further.

It was fun and sensual, and my god, it felt so good just to reconnect with him like this.

"I love you," I murmured into his ear.

He put his hands to my face and pushed me back so I could see him. He was smiling, kiss-swollen lips and a spark in his eyes. "I love you," he mouthed before bringing our mouths back together.

CHAPTER SIX

LAWSON

I COULD KISS JACK FOREVER. Or more to the point, I could have him kiss me forever. There was something to be said about the way he took charge, how he used his strength and his body to remind me that he was mine.

That I was his.

I would have loved for him to have owned me right then and there, in that tent in the cave. But it was neither the place nor the time for *that* level of sexual intimacy. Despite how badly I wanted it.

But having him kiss me like that, to have his weight on me, to have his hands and mouth on me like that, was just as good.

It all simmered down to gentle and tender, sleepy kisses. Jack was warmth and safety, and I almost fell asleep with him on top of me. But eventually he rolled us onto our sides, wrapped me up in his arms, and fell asleep.

I wanted to check on the butterflies, but I wanted this more.

And God only knew how long those butterflies had

inhabited that cave. A decade? A hundred years? A thousand?

I only had my husband like this for one night.

It wasn't a contest.

So wrapped up in his arms, in his love, I closed my eyes and drifted off to sleep.

I AWOKE BEFORE FIVE, and peeling myself away from Jack, I pulled on my boots, coat, and beanie and checked the butterflies on my laptop. They were active, which was utterly confounding to me. Though it shouldn't have been. This butterfly was not exactly nocturnal—it was active during the day making it diurnal. The difference being the cave was pitch black. It thrived in perpetual night, during daylight hours. I knew I'd be researching the variable factors of lepidoptery between night and day, and a species that thrived in the absence of light.

This tiny little creature was about to upend everything we thought we knew about the species.

Everything about its existence, its behaviour—everything that defined it as a butterfly—was different.

It was incredibly exciting.

And I knew this trip to this cave would be the first of a lot in our future. I dreaded being absent from Jack and Brennan for any length of time though. I had no qualms with Jack joining me, his work permitting, of course. But there was no way Brennan could do this. Even considering bringing him on the hike and then abseiling was out of the question.

No, it would mean time away from both of them. And that wasn't something I looked forward to at all.

Or leaving my butterflies in my butterfly house. Or my other research, or my whole life back in Scottsdale, for that matter.

Perhaps I could assign this find to someone else. After my initial report, of course. And after our findings were substantiated and confirmed, of course. I would still have a lot of work to do . . .

"What are you frowning for?" Jack's warm hand rubbed my back.

"Oh. You startled me. I didn't hear you."

"You were miles away," he said gently. "I asked you if something was wrong with the butterflies."

I looked at the screen in front of me. "Oh, no. They're fine. Great, actually. Active at night." The others were still asleep. I didn't want to wake them, so I kept my voice low. "Well, what night is for us. I don't know if the cave eliminates the diurnal and nocturnal barriers, though I can only assume the change in barometric pressure of a night time would play a part. The bats have all mostly returned to roost."

"So why the frown?"

He looked so handsome with his three-day growth. I ran my thumb across it. "I like this," I mumbled.

"Lawson." He used that tone that told me he wasn't interested in vacillation.

"I was just thinking about how much time this will draw me from you and Brennan," I admitted quietly. "And I don't know how much I'm prepared for that. Or even if I'm prepared to do that, at all."

"Lawson, this find is huge. As if all the other work you've done isn't enough to define your career but, my love, this discovery is career-defining."

"I don't care for accolades, Jack. I never have." Then I

shrugged. "Well, except perhaps for the Tillman Copper because my old university professor thought me maladroit."

"This is a lot of big words before—" He checked his watch. "Before 5:00 am, and my first cup of tea. But that tells me you're serious and quite possibly over-thinking things."

"I care for the survival of the species, Jack. That is my number one priority. Facts, research, conservation, longevity. It doesn't matter whose name goes on it. I know my value in this work."

Jack sighed patiently, even smiled a little. "And that's one of the many reasons I love you. But don't make any decisions now. We'll get all the information we can back to the lab, and take it one step at a time." He put his hand to my cheek. "Don't worry about me and Brennan. Our little home on our little farm isn't going anywhere, and if you need to spend time away, we'll be just fine. Don't underestimate how important your work is."

"Don't underestimate how much I don't want to leave. That little house on that little farm is where I belong. With you and our son. Don't underestimate how important that is to me."

"What are you saying, Lawson?"

"I think I might hand this one off. After the initial report, which is still a few months away anyway. I can give a couple of months," I replied. "But I'm busy enough. I can consult and help if they need, but this could turn into years of work and I'm not prepared to miss that much of us. The idea of being away from Brennan for too long makes me feel . . . Is iniquitous the right word?"

The corner of his lip curled upward. "Honestly, I wouldn't know."

I put my hand to my forehead. "Perhaps bereft is more accurate."

He pulled me in for a side-hug and he kissed my temple. "Whatever you decide, you have my full support."

I closed my eyes and allowed myself to lean into him for a brief moment. It dawned on me then that I'd not once doubted his support. He was my absolute rock. "I'm so lucky to have you."

He planted another kiss to the side of my head and rubbed my back. "You only say that because it's my turn to pack up our gear."

I leaned my head on his shoulder. "True."

Jack gave me a playful tap on the backside. "You go pack up your camera and gear in the third chamber." He handed me his torch, then nodded out to the cave entrance where the sky was beginning to lighten. "The sun's about to rise, we've got weather rolling in, and we need to get down this mountain."

I gave a nod and switched the torch on, picked up my backpack, and took it with me into the third chamber. I was careful on my walk through by myself; I'd rather risk running a few minutes late than another sprained ankle or wrist should I fall. But I made my way through to the third chamber without incident. The butterflies all reacted to my entrance, or to the torch, I should say.

There was a ripple of wings across the kaleidoscope. A wave of pink and mauve, almost like they were saying good-bye. "I will be back," I told them softly. "I just want to say that even if I hand this research over, I promise whomever I deem satisfactory will be respectful and non-invasive. We will only return to observe and learn. You have my word."

They didn't answer, of course, though I did receive a few waves in response.

Smiling, I began packing up my gear, making sure it was all fine and stowed in my bag correctly. And with a final glance upward at this absolute marvel of nature, I let them be and made my way back out to the first chamber.

"I had it," Vince was saying. He had his neatly sorted rappelling gear spread out over the cavern floor, his hand was pulling at his hair, his face somewhat pale in the early morning light. "Of course I had it. We used it to get down here."

"Could you have left it up at the bluff?" Amy asked.

Vince shrugged before scrubbing his hand over his face. "No. I mean . . . maybe. I have never left any gear behind. Ever. I'm fastidious. It is ingrained in me, like breathing." He picked up his ropes, clearly looking for something.

Oh, dear.

"What have we misplaced?" I asked, slowly putting my backpack down. I was fairly certain I didn't want to know . . .

Jack gave me a tight smile. "A descender?" he said, sounding unsure about it himself.

Vince let an exasperated sound. "It's a fall arrester. Safety gear. It's a buckle, of sorts, that acts as a brake if you need one. There are two of them, buckled together."

Oh.

"Oh."

"I had it," he said again. "They've got to be here somewhere."

"Can you rig up something instead?" Connor suggested. "I've heard you talk about rigging gear up all the time."

Vince deflated. "I guess. I can make a carabiner brake. It's not my preferred kind, but it's better than nothing." He reached out and picked up a few carabiners, which were a metal buckles that climbers used all the time. Vince had quite a few of them. Then he took one neat bundle of ropes and mumbled to himself, "I'll just need to work out some load bearing and force, rope tensions . . ."

Amy, somewhat stricken, looked at Connor. Connor was staring at Vince. Vince was staring at the ropes in his hand. Jack smiled at me.

"Um, maybe I could help with that," I suggested.

The three of them then stared at me. "Well, it's just physics. When Jack first insisted I go abseiling with him, I was . . . well, horrified. But once I applied physics and worked out a few equations, it's really rather simple."

"Simple?" Connor blinked at me.

"Well, yes." I cleared my throat. "Given we'll need to allow for variances in height and therefore centre of gravity and the angle of the climber's legs in relation to the cliff face, for the sake of this exercise, we can apply the equation to Jack. Factor in his weight of, say eighty-five kilograms and his height of 1.9 metres, and we can assume he has a centre of gravity approximately 1.1 metres from his feet. It would be fair to assume he rappels down the cliff with his body raised thirty degrees above the horizontal. Give or take. If he held the rope approximately 1.4 metres from his feet—" I indicated this position and height using my hands. "—which is fair, given his height, it would make a twenty-degree angle with the cliff face. Give or take. And then we want to find the minimum static coefficient of friction that his feet on the cliff need to have, which will produce the least amount of tension on the rope. We know the force of gravity is vertical, the force of the legs being at thirty degrees multiplied by cosine—"

"Ah, Vince," Amy said, interrupting me mid-explanation. She was holding up a large metal buckle with several lever-type parts. "Is this what you were looking for?"

"Oh my god, yes!" He scrambled to his feet and rushed over to her. "Where was it?"

"Under your tent bag."

"Holy shit." He took the device and held it to his chest. "Thank you."

"Do you think you should maybe not have clipped them together?" Connor asked. "So you could lose one and not both?"

"I didn't think." Vince shook his head, clearly mad at himself. "I just packed everything up together to save space. It was stupid."

"So I can finish explaining the equation if you'd like?" I offered.

Vince grimaced. "Another time, perhaps."

"The answer is approximately 280 newtons," I finished. "Just so you know. Your makeshift braking device would have been more than adequate."

Vince smiled eventually. Connor blinked at me again as though I'd spoken a different language. Amy gave me an approving nod, and Jack . . . well, Jack grinned right at me. "Genius is, genius does."

I ignored the heat in my cheeks. "So, we're ready to leave then?"

Vince was busy sorting out his ropes and harnesses. "Am now."

CHAPTER SEVEN

JACK

THE CLIMB down the mountain wasn't as harrowing as I thought it might be. There were two more decent ledges on the way down, each equipped with rigging bolts for abseiling. It was slow, but it was safe. Vince and Connor were very good at it and put safety over everything.

Lawson, on the other hand, was more worried about his samples and equipment.

I wasn't sure what to make of his announcement to me that he was considering passing this find off to someone else. I was surprised, but maybe I shouldn't have been. Hearing him say he wanted to be home with us more made my heart so damn happy, but I knew his decision to stand down as lead lepidopterist might change.

If he thought for one second the person he'd hand it to wasn't capable, he simply wouldn't hand it over.

If he did decide to stay on board with it, I knew it was going to take up a lot of Lawson's time and focus. And I knew in all likelihood we'd be making this trip a lot in the next few months and possibly exploring other caves in the region. And it was going to be ruling our lives for some time to come.

But I couldn't even be mad about it.

Lawson was rightly excited about this new butterfly, but you know what? I was too.

This was his life's work, and I was a part of his life—butterflies had become such a central part of our lives together—so it was only natural for me to be almost excited as him.

Once we made it down to ground level, with no injuries or damage to any of Lawson's research samples, after we all took a few minutes to use the rainforest "bathroom" in private, we made the hike back to Connor's four-wheel drive and made the rough and bumpy trip through the forest back to where we'd left our SUV.

As great as the trip had been, and as grateful as I was to Connor, Vince, and Amy, I was very relieved to see our car. We unloaded all our gear out of Connor's vehicle into ours, said our rounds of thanks and goodbyes and promises to be in touch—we'd no doubt be seeing them again real soon—and we were on our way home.

It was going to be about a four-hour drive home, and we'd only been in the car for about twenty seconds before Lawson turned in his seat to face me. "Oh my god, Jack," he blurted out like he was suddenly overwhelmed. "There is so much work to do!"

And he talked and talked and talked non-stop about every detail. The butterfly, the remarkable differences, the similarities, the diet, the relationship to the dark, to the lichen, to the bats. He was certain the bats played some part. As did the temperature, the air pressure, the elevation. Maybe other caves in the area had some too. We'd have to explore all of them. There were so many questions.

"I have one question," I asked. He'd taken a much-needed breath, his palm pressed to his forehead. I thought it might be my only chance to get a word in.

"What's that?"

"What are you going to call it?"

Lawson blinked, stared at me, then out the windscreen, then back at me. "I don't know," he whispered. "You name it."

"No, I will not."

"Yes, you can."

"Okay, call it the Lawson."

"Don't be ridiculous."

"Why is that ridiculous?"

"Because it's egotistical and self-serving."

I snorted. "Then you name it."

He sighed, his conversation derailed. "I would need to consider a great deal of factors."

I took his hand and kissed his knuckles, smiling at how much calmer he was now. At least he was breathing normally. "Are you still considering handing it over to someone else?"

He chewed on his bottom lip and stared out the windscreen for a bit, then nodded. "I think so. Once the prelims are done and the groundwork is established. There's still a lot of work in that, but by then the weather will have warmed up and my work at home will be in full swing. I'll have enough to worry about. Plus, I meant what I said. I don't want to be traipsing all over anymore, Jack. I want to be home with you and Brennan."

I kissed his knuckles again. "I love you."

He smiled at me, clearly tired but happy. "And that makes me one very lucky, very happy man. I love you too, Jack."

He scrolled on his phone for a while, sent some emails off to Piers in Queensland, asking him to come at his earliest convenience, then went back to scrolling. He was quiet, reading, researching, double-checking, and we were soon pulling into our driveway. The clouds were low and dark, the weather had turned miserable, but there had never been a prettier sight to me.

Brennan ran out onto the porch, his coat, boots, and beanie on, his grin wide. "Daddas!"

Lawson was out of the car and had him in a big hug before I'd even opened my door. I walked over and collected them both in a big bear hug and said hello to my mum and sister over the top of Lawson's head.

"Did you save the butterflies?" Brennan asked, his brown eyes wide with innocent wonder.

Lawson tweaked his little chubby cheek. "We sure did."

The cold wind snapped around us. "How about we get all of Daddy's gear into his butterfly house, then make hot chocolates and we can tell you all about it?"

We all carried bags, and Brennan carried one with the utmost importance. His daddy's work made him a super-hero according to Brennan, and that was the sweetest thing ever. Raising our son to understand ecology and conservation like he understood colours, shapes, letters, and numbers was never a question. Between my work at the national park and Lawson's butterflies, Brennan was always going to be aware of the world around him.

But then we sat at the dining table, hot chocolates all 'round, and told Mum and Poppy all about the butterfly. Brennan sat on my lap, listening to every word.

Lawson's phone rang and Piers' name appeared on the screen. He flashed me a smile before excusing himself to answer the call.

Mum watched Lawson disappear down the hall. "Life's about to get a whole lot busier," she mused.

"A whole lot better," I corrected gently. I gave Brennan a squeeze. "Daddy's a superhero, isn't he?"

Brennan nodded. "He saves butterflies every day."

Smiling, I kissed the side of his head. "He sure does."

***

Three Months Later

"I finished it," Lawson said nervously as he handed me a copy of his submission to the Australian Lepidopterist Society. His work on the new butterfly had created interest from all over the world. Piers had spent some time here helping him, mostly spending time in Lawson's butterfly house. He wasn't up for the hike or the abseiling, which was understandable.

Lawson and I had made that trek more than a few times in the last three months. We never did find any other specimens in any other caves in the area, but the size and health of the colony led Lawson to believe they might be found in other caves in colder parts of Australia and even New Zealand.

They were out there, just waiting to be found. They just happened to be hiding in places no one would have ever expected to find butterflies. They had taken everything ever known about butterflies and turned it on its head.

Other butterfly enthusiasts were now actively searching their local caves in hopes of finding them. This new species, a remarkable find, had set the Lepidoptera world abuzz, but even further afield, the whole insect and even reptile world had taken note. This was a cold-blooded animal that never saw the sun. It preferred and thrived in absolute darkness in the colder months. Sure, the cave was protected and had a steady climate all year round, but that climate was cold, and this was an exciting find.

Even the lichenology and mycology world was abuzz. The pink lichen turned out to be known in the *Cryptothecia rubrocincta* family, but not in caves and not at these temperatures. It was basically a fungus living off the water source, and the algae and cyanobacteria deterred the bats from eating both the lichen and the butterfly, and the bats protected the butterflies from other predators.

It was such a remarkable symbiosis.

And the butterfly was also, still to this point, nameless.

I'd suggested something to do with the cold or winter. Even something to do with the colour. It was pink, after all. And pink in the animal kingdom was rare.

"But they're not pink," Lawson had argued. "There has been much debate regarding this, as you know."

"Uh, I don't know everything about butterflies like you do, but I know what the colour pink is," I'd replied.

To which Lawson gave me a condensed rundown on structural colourisation. The butterfly was technically purple but appeared pink due to iridescence. They looked pink to me, but I wasn't about to argue the point with Lawson.

Anyway, the newfound butterfly was still nameless. Until now. If he'd finished his submission, which meant he'd given it a name.

I took the folder he'd handed me. He raked his fingers through his hair, patting it down, blinked quickly a few times, and licked his lips. I stood up. "Lawson, my love. What are you nervous about?"

"I'm not nervous," he lied. Then he frowned at the

folder. "I'm not nervous, but if you'd care to read the first page, that would be most appreciated. Put me out of my misery, at least. And if you don't like it or would rather it be called something else, I will understand, but I am of the opinion—"

"Hey," I murmured soothingly. I put my palm to his cheek. "Don't be anxious about it."

Then his expression became one of annoyance. "Would you just please look at it?"

I opened the folder, and under a photograph of the butterfly in question was its name.

The Brighton-Gale Butterfly.

I read the name again and looked at Lawson. He'd put our name on it.

He'd named it after us.

"Lawson . . ."

"If you don't like it—"

"Are you kidding?" I was a little teary, not gonna lie. "I love it. I'm honoured. I'm flattered, and I don't know what to say, to be honest. I'm speechless . . . But you named it after us?"

He nodded. "For you and Brennan." He swallowed hard. "Not for me. I have no need for such things. But for you, because I love you and your support makes my work possible. I couldn't do this without you. You've never questioned the importance of what I do, and I want you to know how much I appreciate that." He blinked back tears. "And for our son. A legacy for him, so in a few hundred years his name will still be remembered."

Sliding the folder onto the table, I took Lawson's face in my hands and kissed him. "I'm so honoured. Thank you. I never expected this. I'm . . . *so honoured*. My heart is so full right now. And I don't think you need to worry about Brennan's legacy. I'm pretty sure he's gonna be saving butterflies when he grows up. You two will be working side by side for a long time."

Lawson gave a teary laugh. "You think so?"

"I know so. And I wouldn't have it any other way."

He hugged me, his face buried in my neck. He nuzzled me for half a second before stopping. "Brennan's asleep, yes?"

I chuckled. "He sure is."

He pulled back and met my gaze. "I've been so busy and it feels like forever since we . . . since you . . ."

I kissed him softly. "Want me to remedy that, Doctor Brighton-Gale?"

"Immediately." He took my hand and led me to our room, closing the door quietly behind us and snicking the lock shut. His eyes were full of fire and love. "Immediately and for as many times as you're able."

I pulled his sweater over his head and pushed him onto the bed. Crawling up his body, I left a trail of butterfly kisses over his skin. His quiet laugh became a moan. "Jack, I'm not a patient man."

I laughed and, like I always had—and like I always would—gave him everything he wanted.

~ the end

ABOUT THE AUTHOR

N.R. Walker is an Australian author, who loves her genre of gay romance. She loves writing and spends far too much time doing it, but wouldn't have it any other way.

She is many things: a mother, a wife, a sister, a writer. She has pretty, pretty boys who live in her head, who don't let her sleep at night unless she gives them life with words.

She likes it when they do dirty, dirty things... but likes it even more when they fall in love.

She used to think having people in her head talking to her was weird, until one day she happened across other writers who told her it was normal.

She's been writing ever since...

ALSO BY N.R. WALKER

Blind Faith

Through These Eyes (Blind Faith #2)

Blindside: Mark's Story (Blind Faith #3)

Ten in the Bin

Gay Sex Club Stories 1

Gay Sex Club Stories 2

Point of No Return – Turning Point #1

Breaking Point – Turning Point #2

Starting Point – Turning Point #3

Element of Retrofit – Thomas Elkin Series #1

Clarity of Lines – Thomas Elkin Series #2

Sense of Place – Thomas Elkin Series #3

Taxes and TARDIS

Three's Company

Red Dirt Heart

Red Dirt Heart 2

Red Dirt Heart 3

Red Dirt Heart 4

Red Dirt Christmas

Cronin's Key

Cronin's Key II

Cronin's Key III

The Dichotomy of Angels

Throwing Hearts

Pieces of You - Missing Pieces #1

Pieces of Me - Missing Pieces #2

Pieces of Us - Missing Pieces #3

Lacuna

Titles in Audio:

Cronin's Key

Cronin's Key II

Cronin's Key III

Red Dirt Heart

Red Dirt Heart 2

Red Dirt Heart 3

Red Dirt Heart 4

The Weight Of It All

Switched

Point of No Return

Breaking Point

Starting Point

Spencer Cohen Book One

Spencer Cohen Book Two

Spencer Cohen Book Three

Yanni's Story

On Davis Row

Evolved

Elements of Retrofit

Clarity of Lines

Sense of Place

Blind Faith

Through These Eyes

Blindside

Finders Keepers

Galaxies and Oceans

Nova Praetorian

Upside Down

Sir

Tallowwood

Imago

Throwing Hearts

Sixty Five Hours

Taxes and TARDIS

The Dichotomy of Angels

The Hate You Drink

Pieces of You

Pieces of Me

Pieces of Us

Free Reads:

Sixty Five Hours

Learning to Feel

His Grandfather's Watch (And The Story of Billy and Hale)

The Twelfth of Never (Blind Faith 3.5)

Twelve Days of Christmas (Sixty Five Hours Christmas)

Best of Both Worlds

Translated Titles:

Fiducia Cieca (Italian translation of Blind Faith)

Attraverso Questi Occhi (Italian translation of Through These Eyes)

Preso alla Sprovvista (Italian translation of Blindside)

Il giorno del Mai (Italian translation of Blind Faith 3.5)

Cuore di Terra Rossa (Italian translation of Red Dirt Heart)

Cuore di Terra Rossa 2 (Italian translation of Red Dirt Heart 2)

Cuore di Terra Rossa 3 (Italian translation of Red Dirt Heart 3)

Cuore di Terra Rossa 4 (Italian translation of Red Dirt Heart 4)

Natale di terra rossa (Red dirt Christmas)

Intervento di Retrofit (Italian translation of Elements of Retrofit)

A Chiare Linee (Italian translation of Clarity of Lines)

Senso D'appartenenza (Italian translation of Sense of Place)

Spencer Cohen 1 Serie: Spencer Cohen

Spencer Cohen 2 Serie: Spencer Cohen

Spencer Cohen 3 Serie: Spencer Cohen

Spencer Cohen 4 Serie: Yanni's Story

Punto di non Ritorno (Italian translation of Point of No Return)

Punto di Rottura (Italian translation of Breaking Point)

Punto di Partenza (Italian translation of Starting Point)

Imago (Italian translation of Imago)

Il desiderio di un soldato (Italian translation of A Soldier's Wish)

Confiance Aveugle (French translation of Blind Faith)

A travers ces yeux: Confiance Aveugle 2 (French translation of Through These Eyes)

Aveugle: Confiance Aveugle 3 (French translation of Blindside)

À Jamais (French translation of Blind Faith 3.5)

Cronin's Key (French translation)

Cronin's Key II (French translation)

Au Coeur de Sutton Station (French translation of Red Dirt Heart)

Partir ou rester (French translation of Red Dirt Heart 2)

Faire Face (French translation of Red Dirt Heart 3)

Trouver sa Place (French translation of Red Dirt Heart 4)

Le Poids de Sentiments (French translation of The Weight of It All)

Lodernde Erde (German translation of Red Dirt Heart)

Flammende Erde 2 (German translation of Red Dirt Heart 2)

Vier Pfoten und ein bisschen Zufall (German translation of Finders Keepers)

Ein Kleines bisschen Versuchung (German translation of The Weight of It All)

Ein Kleines Bisschen Fur Immer (German translation of A Very Henry Christmas)

Weil Leibe uns immer Bliebt (German translation of *Switched*)

Drei Herzen eine Leibe (German translation of *Three's Company*)

Sixty Five Hours (Thai translation)

Finders Keepers (Thai translation)